Clarence M. Barton

Knights of Pythias

Clarence M. Barton

Knights of Pythias

ISBN/EAN: 9783337286767

Printed in Europe, USA, Canada, Australia, Japan

Cover: Foto ©Andreas Hilbeck / pixelio.de

More available books at **www.hansebooks.com**

[SECOND EDITION.]

"ESTO PERPETUA."

KNIGHTS OF PYTHIAS---FOUNDED 1864.

A SKETCH OF THE ORGANIZATION

AND

History of the Knights of Pythias,

To which is annexed the

PROCEEDINGS OF THE GRAND LODGE, D. C., AND PRO-
VISIONAL SUPREME LODGE OF THE UNITED STATES
FOR THE YEAR ENDING JUNE 30TH, 1867.

"Founded on naught but the purest and sincerest motives;
its aim is to alleviate the sufferings of a Brother, succor the unfor-
tunate, zealously watch at the bedside of the sick, soothe the dy-
ing pillow, perform the last sad rites at the grave of a Brother,
offering consolation to the afflicted, and caring for the Widow and
Orphan. Having these principles in view, they will endeavor to
exemplify them by practical tests; and if, by the grace of God,
it shall successfully carry out this object, they will feel that their
mission has not been in vain."

CLARENCE M. BARTON,

Past Grand Chancellor and Grand Recording Scribe

WASHINGTON, D. C.:
R. O. POLKINHORN, PRINTER,
1880.

KNIGHTS OF PYTHIAS.

Perhaps no other charitable organization in the country has labored under greater disadvantages, and brought forth more beneficial results. Organized during the heat of the late civil strife, when society was in a disrupted state, it has steadily advanced in numbers and importance, and is now in a flourishing and prosperous condition. The beautiful lesson of friendship between Damon and Pythias is sought to be *practically* taught by a ritual which, for beauty and perspicuity of language, cannot be surpassed. The strong ties with which the members of the Order are bound together, the interesting and attractive ceremonies of the degrees, the unfailing interest shown for the welfare of the Order, and the generous manner in which the membership have ever responded to the appeals for charity have endeared their hearts more firmly to its principles, and taught them to believe that "true friendship can exist."

As the early history of the Order cannot fail to be interesting, I have collected from the books in possession of the Grand Lodge, sufficient to show its organization and progress.

The first record appearing upon the books of Washington Lodge, No. 1, reads as follows:

WASHINGTON, D. C., *Feb.* 19, 1864.
"AT 'TEMPERANCE HALL,'
"FRIDAY EVENING.

"Upon agreement, a number of gentlemen met, and after some conversation upon the subject, they were called to order, and upon motion of Mr. J. H. RATHBONE a chairman of the meeting was proposed, and Mr. J. T. K. Plant was unanimously called to the chair, and D. L. Burnett nominated as Secretary. After organizing as above, the object of the meeting was stated by Mr. Rathbone to be the organization or foundation of a society, its business and operations to be of a secret character, having for its ultimate object Friendship, Benevolence, and Charity. Before proceeding further, those present were requested to subscribe to an oath laid down afterwards in the Initiatory. All present having signified their willingness to do so, the same was administered to them, by reading the same, by J. H. Rathbone. After the taking of the oath, on motion it was resolved that this Order be styled the *Knights of Pythias.*"

On motion a committee was appointed to prepare a Ritual of opening and closing a Lodge, and of initiation into the same. The Chair appointed as said Committee Brother J. H. Rathbone, who reported a Ritual, which, upon being read, was adopted. After the adoption of the Ritual, the Lodge went into an election for officers, with the following result:

BROTHER J. H. RATHBONE............................. *Worthy Chancellor,*
" JOEL R. WOODRUFF...................... *Vice Chancellor,*
" J. T. K. PLANT............................... *Venerable Patriarch,*
" D. L. BURNETT............................. *Worthy Scribe,*
" A. VAN DER VEER......................... *Banker,*
" R. A. CHAMPION........................... *Assistant Banker,*
" GEORGE R. COVERT....................... *Assistant Scribe.*

The following officers were appointed by the Worthy Chancellor: Brothers M. H. Van Der Veer as Worthy Guide, A. Roderigue as Inside Steward, and as choral Knights, Brothers Kimball, Roberts, D. L. and W. H. Burnett.

On motion the Worthy Chancellor appointed the following Committee to prepare a Ritual for the first degree, (now the second degree,) signs, &c.: Brothers Kimball, Champion, and W. H. Burnett, V. P. J. T. K. Plant, and W. C. J. H. Rathbone as Chairman, added. Committees were then appointed to procure regalias, appliances, &c, after which the first meeting of the Order adjourned to meet again on the evening of the 23d of the same month to perfect the organization.

At the next meeting (on the 23d) the Committee on Degree Ritual presented a report, which was adopted and ordered to be the will of the Lodge and the committee discharged.

The various committees appointed at the previous meeting also reported, and a committee was appointed to procure a seal.

At the next meeting (27th of February) various applications were received for membership. It also appears that at this meeting a committee of three, consisting of V. C. Woodruff, W. C. Rathbone, and Brother D. L. Burnett was appointed to prepare a Ritual of the Second (now the third) Degree, which was soon after prepared by the committee, presented to the Lodge and adopted.. At the meeting on the 24th of March; the Lodge proceeded to an election for officers to serve the ensuing quarter, and in addition to the officers elected, Brothers Woodruff, M. A. Van Der Veer, and Roderigue were elected Representatives to the Grand Lodge, which was organized on the 8th of April by members of Washington Lodge. On the 21st of April, at a regular meeting of Washington Lodge, Brother J. H. Rathbone's resignation of office and membership in the Order was presented, read, and accepted.

Brother Rathbone, at the time of his resignation, occupied the position of Venerable Patriarch, he having been the first Chancellor of Washington Lodge. The fact of being a Past Chancellor, it would seem, did not require him to fill the office of Venerable Patriarch, for after his resignation was received and accepted, the Lodge went into an election to fill the vacancy, and Brother D. L. Burnett, formerly a Scribe of the Lodge, was elected and duly installed into the office. The minutes of the Lodge up to this time indicate that the office of Venerable Patriarch was the third office in the Lodge, the duties of which were to deliver the obligations and open and close the Lodge with prayer. The Degrees were at this time known as the Initiatory and First and Second Degrees.

The Grand Lodge, which was organized on the 8th of April, with J. T. K. Plant as Grand Chancellor, and A. Van Der Veer as Grand Scribe, set about forming Lodges elsewhere, and providentially succeeded in locating one at the Navy Yard, known as Franklin Lodge, No. 2, with the following Charter members:

ROBERT I. MIDDLETON...................... *Venerable Patriarch,*
DANIEL CARRIGAN......... .... *Worthy Chancellor,*
EDW. FOX... *Vice-Chancellor,*
CLARENCE M. BARTON..................... .... *Scribe,*
JAMES GILL....................................... *Banker,*
NICHOLAS WAYSON........................... *Guide,*
JOS. H. LAWRENCE........................... *Inner Steward,*
HUDSON PETTIT.............................. *Outer Steward,*
Edward Dunn, James W. Kelly, Jasper Scott, George Norton, J. H. Wheeler.

The Lodge was duly instituted on the 12th of April, at the Ana-costia Engine House, by the officers of the Grand Lodge.

The history of this Lodge needs no comment. It is the history of the Order, which it saved from destruction after her sister Lodges around her had ceased to exist. From its very organization the members took a lively interest in its welfare, and determined that it should become the "Excelsior Lodge" of the Order. For nearly eight months it struggled along, the only Lodge of the Order in the country; its little membership meeting with rebuffs and sarcasms, and worse than this, the stinging sin of ingratitude from the hands of one who had solemnly sworn to maintain and defend its principles.

On the 19th of May, 1864, the Grand Lodge organized Columbia Lodge, No. 3, located at Temperence Hall; on the 2d of June, Potomac Lodge, No. 4, was also organized at Temperance Hall, and afterwards located at Island Hall, on the Island; on the 1st of February, 1865, Alexandria Lodge, No. 1, of Virginia, was organized through the efforts of Brother John H. King, of Franklin Lodge, then engaged in the United States naval service near Alexandria. Brother King was appointed Deputy Grand Chancellor of the State of Virginia.

The Lodges were at this time in a bad financial condition, but doing as well as could be expected under the circumstances. Potomac and Columbia Lodges ceased holding meetings in the latter part of April in consequence of being unable to secure a quorum; the minutes of Washington Lodge also show that for months at a time no meetings were held, in consequence of not being able to secure the number of members necessary to transact business. Alexandria Lodge ceased holding meetings in July, and at the annual session of the Grand Lodge in June, 1865, but two Lodges were represented, Washington and Franklin.

At that session the following Grand Officers were elected and installed:

CLARENCE M. BARTON....No. 2.........*Grand Chancellor,*		
JOSEPH H. LAWRENCE.... 2.........*Vice Grand Chancellor,*		
EDWARD DUNN............ 2.........*Grand Marshal,*		
WM. WHITNEY.............. 1.......... " *Scribe,*		
Dr. J. R. KEASBEY.......... 1.......... " *Banker,*		
JOHN W. CROSS............. 2.......... " *Herald,*		
A. VAN DER VEER.......... 1.......... " *Prelate,*		
R. V. HENRY............... 1.......... " *Inner Guardian,*		
J. TITCOMB................ 1.......... " *Outer* "		

The Grand Lodge held its last session on the 13th of June, 1865; Washington Lodge, No. 1, ceased holding meetings in July of the same year, and petitioned Franklin Lodge to receive the members who were in good standing at the dissolution of the Lodge, which was done a short while afterward. A few of them were members of Potomac Lodge that had been received in membership in a similar manner by Washington Lodge. Franklin Lodge, No. 2, upon the 1st of August, 1865, was the only Lodge in existence, the Grand Lodge having become defunct from necessity—it not being deemed advisable to continue its organization with but one Subordinate Lodge. Franklin Lodge, however, exercised all the functions of a Grand Lodge, its past officers installing the newly elected officers of their Lodge each quarter. The work, regalia, &c., in possession of Washington Lodge at the time of its decease, was turned over to Franklin Lodge on the 28th of September, upon the payment of $18.75, the sum necessary to pay one quarter's rent of hall due by that Lodge.

At the close of the year 1865 Franklin Lodge was in a prosperous condition, with a membership of nearly sixty, and nearly $200 in the treasury. They had sustained a loss during the year, through their Banker, of $255.55.

At the beginning of the year 1866 the membership made a determined effort to either resuscitate the old Lodges or establish new ones. The business of the Order had heretofore been conducted in the Knight's Degree, but by resolution of the Lodge, on the 5th of March, "it was ordered that after the last meeting in that month all business, except the conferring degrees, should be done in the Page Degree." During this month the Constitution of the Lodge was revised, and two hundred copies printed and circulated. The funds on hand at the expiration of the first quarter in 1866 were still very small, amounting to but $123.45.

At a regular meeting, April 2, Financial Scribe Thomas Hamilton moved that a committee of five be appointed to canvass the city for purpose of organizing a new Lodge of the Order. The following Committee was appointed: Brothers Hamilton, Lawson, Cook, King, and Schlief. At the next regular meeting, April 9, the Committee reported having procured fifteen names in favor of forming a new Lodge, and on the next meeting night, 18th of April, a Charter was granted Mount Vernon Lodge, No. 5, by the past Chancellors of Franklin Lodge, and the members duly initiated and instructed in the rites and ceremonies of the Order. The following officers of this Lodge were installed:

JOHN I. DOWNS...................................*Venerab'e Patriarch,*
WM. L. CHILDS.................................. *Worthy Chancellor,*
JOHN DAUGHTON............................... *Vice*   "
GEORGE SCHULTZ...............................*Recording Scribe,*
RICHARD T. SEARS............................. *Financial*   "
JOHN GRIGGS................................... *Banker,*
WM. A. COOPER................................. *Guide,*
CHARLES GARDINER........................·····...........*Inner Steward,*
JOHN BAUMAN.................................. *Outer*   "

The installation work was revised, and a committee appointed to prepare a design for regalia. A committee was also appointed to write copies of the Ritual for Mount Vernon Lodge.

The Ritual in use at the time, and from the foundation of the Order, was in manuscript, and in but few respects like the present one. At the close of each degree there were no charges or lecture, save an impromptu lecture at the close of the Second Degree, then styled the First. The grips, signs, &c., were imperfect, and the obligations but repetitions of each other.

On the 30th of April, 1865, the following petition was received in Franklin Lodge:

"WASHINGTON, D. C.

"FRANKLIN LODGE, No 2.

"OFFICERS AND BROTHERS:

"I respectfully make application for membership in Franklin Lodge, No. 2. Having been the sole originator of the Order, and a member in good standing of Washington Lodge, No. 1. now defunct, I make this application from a pure love of the Order and a desire to see it prosper; and I wish to devote my energies to the above purpose.

"Respectfully yours in F. C. and B.,

"P. C. J. H. RATHBONE."

P. C's J. W. Cross, King, and Barton as a committee examined the application, reported favorable, and it was unanimously received.

P. C's Dunn, Cross, and Barton then conducted Brother Rathbone into the Lodge, introducing him to the W. C. and members. Upon invitation Brother Rathbone then gave a history of the organization of the Order, his connection with it in 1864, and his reason for resigning his office and membership, &c.

The need of a perfect Ritual, in order to make the ceremonies more interesting and attractive, had long been felt, and at this meeting of the Lodge the following Committee was appointed to revise the Ritual, and if possible report at the next meeting night: Past Chancellors, Rathbone, Barton, Dunn, Cross, Cook, F. S. Lawson, and Brother Cooksey of Franklin Lodge, and F. S. Sears and V. P. Downs of Mount Vernon Lodge. On the 14th of May the committee reported that the Ritual had been placed, by their sanction, in the hands of Brother Rathbone for revision, and that he had performed his duty and reported to the committee, who had unanimously approved of it. The report of the committee was received and adopted, and the Ritual now in use was read and adopted as the Ritual of the Order, by Franklin and Mount Vernon Lodges in joint meeting. It was also resolved at this meeting to reorganize the Grand Lodge.

REORGANIZATION OF THE GRAND LODGE.

On the 1st of May, 1866, pursuant to agreement, Past Chancellors Rathbone, Barton, Dunn, King, Cook, and Beech, of No. 2, John I. Downs, of No. 5, and Representative Stromberger, of No. 5, met for the purpose of reorganizing the Grand Lodge, which had held no meetings since June, 1865. The offices of Grand Marshal, Herald, Prelate, and Inner and Outer Guardian, in vogue at that time, were discontinued, and the following officers were elected:

J. H. RATHBONE.............................. *Grand Chancellor,*
EDW. DUNN................................... *Vice Grand "*
CLARENCE M. BARTON.................... *Grand Recording Scribe,*
JOHN I. DOWNS............................. " *Financial* "
JOHN H. KING.............................., ... " *Banker,*
THOMAS W. COOK.......................... " *Guide,*
LEVI BEECH................................. " *Inner Steward,*
JOHN W. CROSS............................. " *Outer* "

On motion of G. R. S. Barton, the office of V. G. P. was made an appointive office for the first three months. The above officers were elected to serve the unexpired term of those whose tenure-of-office had ceased when the Grand Lodge became defunct in June, 1865—the term expiring in June, 1866. At this meeting the signs, grips, passwords, &c.; of the old work were changed by G. C. Rathbone, a secret cypher established, and a committee appointed to have the Rituals printed.

The next meeting was held on 28th of May, all the officers being present except the G. O. S. Three Representatives from No. 5, Brothers Downey, Jordon, and Stromberger, were also present.

A committee was appointed to draft a Constitution, By-Laws, and Installation work; also one to secure a design for a charter and diploma of Subordinate Lodge members, and Regalia for Grand Lodge members.

Joseph H. Lawrence, of No. 2, was appointed V. G. P. to serve the balance of the term.

P. G. C. J. T. K. Plant was expelled from the Order for divers reasons known to members of the Order. P. C. John H. King was appointed a committee of one to negotiate for and buy the work of the defunct Lodge in Alexandria.

An ineffectual attempt was also made at this meeting to declare null and void the proceedings of the old Grand Lodge, and change the numbers of Franklin and Mount Vernon Lodges to Nos. 1 and 2, respectively.

JUNE 4, 1866.

All the officers were present at this meeting, except the G. C., G. G., and G. I. S.

P.C. KING offered a form of application to establish new Lodges, which was adopted.

P. C. KING offered a design for apron-regalia for Subordinate Lodges, which was adopted. A communication was ordered to be sent to J. T. K. Plant, requesting him to deliver up the books, seal, and papers of the Grand Lodge.

A communication was read from Franklin Lodge, turning over to the Grand Lodge all the property of defunct Lodges in its possession, for the sum of $18.75, payable in three months time.

P. C. BARTON moved that the Grand Lodge transfer to Mount Vernon Lodge all the working material then in her possession. The motion was lost.

On motion, it was ordered that the V. P. of Subordinate Lodges be an appointed officer for the first term only, and all new Lodges be allowed four Representatives the first quarter, and three Representatives the three following quarters.

JUNE 18, 1866.

At this session P. C. John W. Cross declined to serve as G. O. S., which declination was received.

The new constitution and by-laws of the Grand Lodge were reported by the committee, and V. G. C. Dunn was appointed a committee to draft form of processions.

On motion, duly seconded, it was ordered "that in Subordinate Lodges the V. C. shall be addressed by all persons wishing to leave the room before the adjournment of the Lodge."

It was then ordered that the first annual and quarterly session of the Grand Lodge, for the coming fiscal year, be held at the room of Franklin Lodge, No. 2, on the second Monday in July.

Thus closed the last meeting held in the unexpired term—the Grand Lodge having in its possession the sum of sixty-one dollars—sixty of which had been loaned to her by the two Lodges, Franklin and Mount Vernon.

ANNUAL AND QUARTERLY SESSION.

JULY 9, 1866.

The Grand Lodge met in due form. Absent, G. C., G. G., G. I. S., and G. O. S. The credentials of P. C. Childs, and Representatives Stromberger, D. and B. Daughton, of No. 5, were received. The quarterly reports of Nos. 2 and 5 Lodges were then presented; No. 2 showed a membership of 43; General Fund, $112.16; Widow and Orphan Fund, $8.14; percentage, $7.13. No. 5 a membership of 96; General Fund, $222.54; Widow and Orphan Fund, $32.26; percentage, $22.25.

Mount Vernon Lodge has thus far been a complete success, and the manner in which their membership worked to extend the Order and its principles cheered those who had been so long engaged in its behalf to renewed exertions. The Grand Lodge, too, began to feel that she has something to rely upon, and determined to put forth a stronger effort than ever before to advance the work.

At this session the following Grand Officers were elected to serve for one year:

EDWARD DUNN............No. 2............		*Grand Chancellor.*
JOHN I. DOWNS............	5............	*Vice Grand* "
CLARENCE M. BARTON....	2............	*Grand Recording Scribe,*
W. L. CHILDS...............	5............	" *Financial* "
JOHN H. KING...............	2............	" *Banker,*
JASPER SCOTT...............	2............	" *Guide,*
R. V. HENRY...............	2............	" *Inner Steward,*
THOMAS W. COOK..........	2............	" *Outer* "

Past Grand Chancellor J. H. Rathbone succeeded to the Chair of Venerable Grand Patriarch, now made the highest office in the Grand Lodge. P. C. John H. King reported having negotiated for and purchased the work of the defunct Alexandria Lodge for $33.50 ; which sum was ordered to be paid. The P. C's report was received, and the committee discharged from further consideration of the subject. The following resolution was passed :

"*Resolved*, That all sums received from members of new Lodges, constituting them chartered members, are to be considered as received for initiation and degree fees."

SPECIAL SESSION.

\ JULY 12, 1866.

The following business was transacted at this session. The new printed Ritual was placed in the hands of a committee of three, P. C's Fox, Dunn and King, and compared with the manuscript work. After the correction of a few typographical errors, the original manuscript was destroyed by fire. A communication was ordered to be sent to the two Lodges, requiring them to deliver up their manuscript Ritual, and receive in lieu five copies of the printed, free of expense. The supply standard was placed at five copies for $20. A Lodge applying for the second set to be furnished at $10.

On motion it was ordered that one card of the secret cypher be transmitted to the W. C. of each Lodge to transfer it quarterly to his successor. A bill of $57.50 was then presented for printing, examined by Finance Committee, and ordered to be paid.

JULY 16, 1866.

An adjourned annual and quarterly session was held. The manuscript work from the two Lodges were delivered to the Grand Lodge by the P. C., and a committee appointed to destroy them ; which was done. A design for a charter, executed by P. C. John H. King, was exhibited, and a committee of four appointed to perfect the design for charter and diploma. Committee—P. C's King and Barton, and Representatives Daughton and Stromberger.

JULY 30, 1866.

A special session was held—P. G. C. Rathbone in the chair. A petition for a charter was received, with forty-three signers, to or-

2

ganize Liberty Lodge, No. 6, to be located at the Navy Yard. The following were the officers of the Lodge:

WM. P. WESTWOOD............................ *Venerable Patriarch,*
THOMAS E. PYLES............................ *Worthy Chancellor,*
JOHN T. SMITH............................ *Vice* "
A. C. HOOPS............................ *Recording Scribe,*
JAMES MATTHIESON............................ *Financial* "
SAMUEL LANGLEY..............................*Banker,*
ALONZA SHAW............................ *Guide,*
WM. SISSELL............................ *Inner Steward,*
W. HARDY............................ *Outer* "

The charter was granted, and the gentlemen, being in waiting, were introduced and instructed in the mysteries of the Order.

AUGUST 8, 1866.

A special session was held—G. C. Edw. Dunn in the chair. P. C. Barton was appointed a committee of one to inquire into cost of printed charters.

On motion it was ordered "that the W. C. of each Subordinate Lodge should be notified that the printed Ritual should never be removed from the Lodge room, but should be open at any time, in the Lodge room, for perusal by any Knight in good standing."

The following was established as the working regalia of Subordinate Lodges : for Knights, plain red collar ; Esquires, yellow collar; Pages, blue collar; for officers, plain red collar, with movable insignia of office upon them ; for V. P., plain black collar, with Bible in metal upon it.

It was resolved that the apron-regalia, which was established at this session, should never be worn in the Lodge room, except in visiting or receiving sister Lodges, official visitation, and funerals.

The installation work of the Grand Lodge was here read by P. G. C. Rathbone, and adopted. The funeral services were also read and adopted, and P. G. C. Rathbone appointed to add a short prayer. P. C. Childs was appointed a committee to get up design for apron-regalia of Grand Lodge officers and members.

AUGUST 20, 1866.

A special session was held, G. C. Edw. Dunn in the Chair. The Committee on G. L. Officers' and members' regalia submitted a report, which was adopted, and the apron-regalia (now in use) made the established regalia of the Grand Lodge.

The Committee on inquiring into the cost of printing charters submitted a report, when P. C's Barton and Cross were authorized to have fifty printed.

The following resolution was adopted :

"*Resolved*, That, in order to more fully instruct candidates in the mysteries of the Order, not more than six be allowed to be initiated and instructed in the several degrees at one time."

APPROPRIATIONS—$10 to Committee on Charters ; $5 to P. C. John H. King for Charters.

AUGUST 24, 1866.

•An application for a charter was presented to the Grand Chancellor to organize Webster Lodge, No. 7, signed by Harry Kronheimer, David Nachman, I. L. and H. L. Blout, E. Voight, D. L. Demelman, C. W. Okey, Wolf Kaufman, J. Peyser, P. Peyser, and others. The charter was granted, and the Lodge organized on the 27th by the Grand Lodge Officers, at Franklin Lodge room.

AUGUST 29, 1866.

A special meeting was held, P. C, Edw. Dunn in the Chair. A committee of three—P. C. Barton, Representatives Daughton and Stromberger—was appointed to procure a suitable hall for the meetings of the Grand Lodge.

Webster Lodge, No. 7, was loaned a full set of working material until the Grand Lodge should require it. An invitation was read and accepted from Mount Vernon Lodge, No. 5, to be present at their excursion to Mount Vernon and Glymont.

The burgee (now in use) was adopted, and P. C's Scott, Childs, and King appointed a committee to procure the burgee and lance.

The following resolution was adopted :

"That, hereafter, when a person applies for membership in a Lodge outside of his jurisdiction, a communication shall be sent to the Lodge nearest his residence asking for his character."

Webster Lodge was allowed to keep their charter open until the 21st of October.

APPROPRIATIONS.—$15 to Franklin Lodge to reimburse her for outlay for blanks, &c.; $1 for room rent.

SEPTEMBER 7, 1866.

An adjourned special session was held at Temperance Hall, G. C., Edw. Dunn in the Chair.

The Committee on Securing Hall reported having procured Temperance Hall at $3 per meeting night. The report was received. The following committees were appointed :

Election and Returns—P. C.'s Barton, Martin, and Losano. *On Grievance*—P. C's Cross, Henry, and Childs. *On Supervision*—P. C's Fox, Scott, and Childs.

Franklin Lodge, No. 2, requested that her charter be re-opened until fifty additional members be secured, each candidate to be admitted in a constitutional form, and be disqualified from receiving benefits for six months. The request occasioned considerable debate; after which it was granted, with the following amendment : " That hereafter no Lodge shall be allowed to open its charter after being once closed."

The Committee on Apron-Regalia reported having procured samples of the same from the manufacturers, and presented bills. The report was received and the committee discharged from the further consideration thereof. The following appropriations were made :

Hall Rent	$3 00
To Finish Burgee	10 00
Apron-Regalias (sample)	28 25
Total	$41 25

REGULAR QUARTERLY SESSION.

OCTOBER 8, 1866.

G. C. Edw. Dunn in the Chair. The proceedings of the previous quarterly and special sessions were read and approved. The credentials of the following Past Chancellors and Representatives were presented :

Thomas Hamilton, of No. 2 ; R. T. Johnson, of No. 5 ; W. P. Westwood and Thomas E. Pyles, of No. 6 ; Harry Kronheimer and I. L. Blout, of No. 7. Representatives, John Daughton, John M. Mitchel and Josiah Gray, of No. 5 ; W. P. Allen, William Ready, and L. A. Tuell, of No. 6 ; H. L. Blout, J. Pyser, and C. W. Okey, of No. 7 ; which were referred to the Committee on Election and Returns, reported favorable thereon, and recommended their admission, which was concurred in. The Past Chancellors and Representatives Gray, Allen, Ready, Tuell, Blout, and Okey were then admitted and obligated.

The Committee on Burgee reported the same completed, at a cost of $10 ; the report was received, the committee discharged, and the burgee placed in the hands of Grand Banker King for the Grand Lodge.

P. C. Barton stated that he had in his possession a new Constitution which he had prepared, in view of the fact that the one in use was not sufficient to meet the demand for the proper government of the Lodges. The Constitution was, upon motion of P. C. R. T. Johnson, read by articles and sections, and had been read as far as article VIII, section V, when the Grand Lodge adjourned until the thirteenth.

Table showing the condition of the Lodges at the close of the quarter ending September 30, 1866.

	MEMBERSHIP.						General Fund.	School, or Widow and Orphan Fund.	Total on hand.	Total expended.	Paid for relief of sick.	Paid for the burying of Brothers.	Per centage.
	Pages.	Esquires.	Knights.	Past Chancellors.	P. G. C.'s.	Total.							
No. 2, Franklin............	6	2	35	12	1	57	$191 49	$22 32	$231 81	$52 50	$24 00	......	$12 75
No. 5, Mount Vernon.....	......	......	92	3	......	95	118 81	44 42	170 44	209 61	20 00	$39 00	10 58
No. 6, Liberty.............	1	2	149	1	......	153	271 00	52 82	323 82	204 43	......	......	47 54
No. 7, Webster............	1	......	17	1	......	19	8 41	9 50	17 91	68 54	......	......	8 55
	7	5	293	17	1	324	$589 71	$129 06	$743 98	$535 08	$44 00	$39 00	$79 42

Total Membership 324.

OCTOBER 13, 1866.

The Grand Lodge met in due form, pursuant to adjournment—G. C. Edw. Dunn in the chair. Representative John Daughton, of No. 5, was admitted and instructed The new constitution was again taken up, and the remaining articles and sections adopted ; and the constitution adopted in whole. The Representatives from No. 6 moved that hereafter the Committee on the Good of the Order be appointed in open Lodge; adopted.

P. C's Childs, Barton, and Representative Okey were appointed a committee to inquire into the expediency of having the constitution printed. At this session G. R. S. Clarence M. Barton requested that his rank in the Order be more clearly defined, he having been elected Grand Chancellor of the Order in June, 1865, and remaining as such until the Grand Lodge ceased its functions by the decease of all the Lodges, except Franklin. After debate upon the matter, it was resolved that P. C. Clarence M. Barton be known hereafter as a Past Grand Chancellor of the Order. The Grand Lodge then adjourned until 16th October.

OCTOBER 16, 1866.

Pursuant to adjournment, the Grand Lodge met in due form— G. C. Edw. Dunn in the chair. Representative Jacob Peyser, of No. 7, was admitted and instructed. P. C. Edw. Fox applied for the honors of a Past Grand Chancellor. After debate, the subject was laid on the table. Brothers J. Peyser, I. L. Blout, and Tuell were appointed a committee to have the funeral services printed. The following article was offered and read:

"That the Subordinate Lodges shall do all their work in the Knight Degree."

A motion was made to suspend the rules to take up the article for action upon it. The Chair decided the motion not in order. An appeal was taken from the decision of the Chair, and the chair was sustained. The Grand Lodge then adjourned.

NOVEMBER 22, 1866.

A special session was held—P. G. C. Barton in the Chair. The parts of the Constitution conflicting with the Ritual were taken up and stricken out. P. C's Barton, Westwood, and Kronheimer were appointed a committee to procure the officers rosettes and emblems. The same committee was appointed to get up a design for working regalia of Grand Lodge.

The Committee on Funeral Services presented prayer, which was read and adopted. Adjourned.

DECEMBER 28, 1866.

A special session was held—G. C. Edw. Dunn in the Chair. The By-Laws of the subordinate Lodges were presented and read by the G. R. S. The parts conflicting with the Constitution and Ritual were sticken out, and the By-Laws adopted; P. C's Barton, Martin, and Kronheimer were appointed a committee to examine the proof-sheets, and compare them with the original manuscript. Adjourned.

REGULAR QUARTERLY SESSION.

JANUARY 14, 1867.

The Grand Lodge met in due form, at Temperance Hall—V. G. C. John I. Downs in the Chair, The minutes of the last quarterly, adjourned, and special sessions were read and approved. The credentials of the following Past Chancellors and Representatives were presented, and referred to the Committee on Election and Returns, who reported favorable thereon, and recommended their admission.

Past Chancellors—D. Carrigan and R. T. Lawson, of No. 2; R. T. Sears, of No.5; John T. Smith, of No. 6; H. L. Blout, of No. 7. Representatives—F. Stromberger, Jno. E. Herrell, and W. F. Garrett, of No. 5; Stephen Simonds, F. Prosperi, and Wm. Ready, of No. 6; J.Peyser, Thos. Rich, and C. W. Okey, of No. 7.

Past Chancellors Carrigan, Smith, Sears, and Lawson, and Representatives Herrell, Garrett, Simonds, and Rich were admitted and instructed.

The committee also examined the quarterly reports, and reported favorably thereon. The report of No. 7 was not presented.

The Committee on Funeral Service reported having it printed, and presented a bill for the same; and they were discharged from the further consideration of the subject.

The Committee on Officers' Rosettes reported having secured them at a cost of $8.

The Committee on Working Regalia for Grand Lodge members submitted a report ; and after debate it was laid upon the table.

The Committee on inquiring into the cost and expediency of having the Grand Lodge Constitution printed submitted a report, that they could have one hundred copies printed at a cost of $32, and deem it expedient to have them printed at once.

P. G. C. Barton offered the following resolution.

"*Resolved*, That hereafter, on the night of installation, the Worthy Chancellor of each Lodge shall appoint four officers, styled 'Attendants,' to serve during the quarter, and to be fined in the case of absence—said Attendants to assist the officers of the Lodge during the Initiation and conferring of the Degrees."

After debate upon the resolution, the yeas and nays were called, and it was adopted by the following vote: Yeas—Past Chancellors Carrigan, Barton, Smith, Lawson, Cross, Childs, Westwood, Fox, Downs, Henry, Sears, and Beach.—Representatives, Simonds, Rich, Stromberger, Jacob Peyser, and Herrell. Nays—Past Chanclleors Johnson, Pyles, and Hamilton, and Representative Garrett.

The following resolution was offered and unanamously adopted:

"That, hereafter, previous to the installation of the Banker of Subordinate Lodges, he will be required to deliver the funds of the Lodge to his successor, in the presence of the installing Officer."

The motion passed by the Grand Lodge on 7th of September, 1866, to prevent the charter of any Lodge from being opened after it had been closed, was then, upon motion, reconsidered, and on motion of P. C. John W. Cross, Webster Lodge, No. 7, was allowed to reopen her charter for the space of one year, and confer the Page, Esquier, and Knight Degrees for the sum of $5. P. C's Carrigan, Westwood, and Barton were appointed a committee to revise the installation work of Subordinate Lodges. P. C. Thomas Hamilton stated that he had collected a sum of money for the purpose of paying the necessary expenses to establish a Lodge of the order in Pennsylvania. The list of names of those subscribing were presented by the P. C. The G. C. was empowed to pay over the amount to those who might be deputized to organize a Lodge outside the district. The following appropriations were made:

Printing Constitution of Grand Lodge...................................$32 00
Rosettes for Officers... 8 00
Printing Funeral Odes... 3 50
Hall Rent... 3 00

Total...$40 50

The Grand Lodge adjourned until the 29th instant.

Table showing the condition of the Subordinate Lodges, for the Quarter ending December 31, 1866.

Names	Membership							Received during quarter.				Expended during quarter.				On hand.				Per Centage to Grand Total
	Increase	Decrease	Pages	Esquires	Knights	P.C's.	P.G.C's	General Fund.	School Fund.	Special Tax.	Total.	Relief of Sick.	Funerals.	Relief of Distress.	Total Expended.	General Fund.	Widow and Orphan, or School Fund.	Special Tax.	Total.	
No. 2, Franklin	24	1	8		57	12	2	$167.09	$18.56		$185.65	$4.00		$2.50	$140.40	$218.12	$40.28		$259.00	$16.70
No. 5, Mount Vernon	9	2	5	2	90	4		138.15	15.35	$74.50	228.00	32.00	$70.00	25.00	311.13	84.13	39.37	$82.11	205.61	13.81
No. 6, Liberty	9		4	1	157	3		214.73	196.97	168.00	569.70			15.00	410.94	161.91	249.79	158.00	569.70	22.24
No. 7, Webster	12				31	3		79.58	8.83		88.38*				49.13	47.66	18.33		65.99	7.95
	54	3	17	3	335	22	2	$599.55	$239.71	$232.50	$1,071.73	$36.00	$70.00	$42.50	$911.66	$511.82	$347.77	$240.11	$1,100.30	$50.70

JANUARY 29, 1867.

The Grand Lodge met pursuant to adjournment, at Union Lodge Hall, and was opened in due form—G. C. Edw. Dunn in the chair.

The credentials of Representative Darnell, of No. 6, were received, examined, and the brother admitted and instructed.

The Committee on Printing reported having received twenty copies of the Grand Lodge Constitution, the remainder to be finished in a few days. The report was received.

The Committee, on comparing the proof sheets of the Constitution and By-Laws of Subordinate Lodges with the original manuscript, reported that the proofs were examined by them and found to be filled with errors. They asked to be discharged; which was agreed to.

The Committee on Grand Lodge Working-Regalia submitted three different plans for consideration, and, after discussion, the following was adopted as the working-regalia of the Grand Lodge: Past Grand Chancellors and Venerable Grand Patriarchs, black velvet collars, trimmed with gold. The letters P. G. C. worked in gold on the former, and a Bible in gold on the latter. For all officers and Past Chancellors, a red velvet collar, trimmed with gold bullion. On the officers' collars their insignia will be worked in gold; for Representatives from Subordinate Lodges, a red velvet collar, trimmed with silver bullion.

The Committee on getting up a form of installation for Subordinate Lodges (P. C's Carrigan, Barton, and Westwood) submitted a form, which was read, (the same now in use,) and, after a lengthy discussion, adopted by a vote of eleven to five.

The seats of Grand Guide, Jasper Scott, and Grand Inner Steward, R. V. Henry, were declared vacant according to the Constitution, they having been absent six sessions.

The Grand Lodge went into an election, and P. C. W. P. Westwood, of No. 6, was elected Grand Guide, and P. C. R. T. Johnson, of No. 5, Grand Inner Steward. Representative Herrell, of No. 5, asked the following interrogatories:

"1. Is it lawful to assess the members of a Lodge $1 a head on the decease of a Brother, and turn the same into the Treasury of the Lodge when there is no widow or children to receive it?

"2. Has a Lodge a right to levy a tax on its members for any object not specified in the Constitution and By-Laws of said Lodge?"

The interrogatories, after a lengthy debate, were referred to the Grievance Committee.

In reply to a question by Representative Stromberger, the Grand Chancellor decided that members of Subordinate Lodges had no right to know the business transacted by the Grand Lodge, unless officially informed of it.

After the transaction of other business, the Grand Lodge adjourned until 12th of February.

The following appropriations were made :

To Mount Vernon Lodge, for money loaned.............................$30 00
To Hall Rent.. 5 00

FEBRUARY 12, 1867.

The Grand Lodge met pursuant to adjournment, and was opened in due form—G. C. Edw. Dunn in the Chair.

The credentials of Representative H. V. Cole, of No. 7, vice Thos. Rich, resigned, were received, examined, and the brother admitted and instructed. G. G. Westwood and G. I. S. Johnson were duly installed in office.

The Committee on Printing Grand Lodge Constitution made a partial report, and asked for an appropriation of $3 to supply deficiency. The report was received.

The Committee on Rosettes and Emblems reported having procured the emblems at a cost of $16, and were discharged from the further consideration of the subject.

On motion of P. C. Daniel Carrigan, a copy of the printed Ritual, with the seal attached, was loaned to P. G. C. J. H. Rathbone until such times as the Grand Lodge should demand it.

The Grievance Committee, P. C's John W. Cross and R. V. Henry, to whom had been referred the interrogatories of Representative Herrell, on the 29th of January, reported as to the first interrogatory, "That no tax could be levied;" and as to the second, "That a Lodge has a right to levy a tax for any purpose not specified in the Constitution and By-Laws; provided it be done by unanimous consent of those present."

P. C. MARTIN moved that the report of the committee be received and adopted. After discussion upon the subject, and various motions and appeals, P. G. C. Barton moved that the whole subject be postponed until the next session of the Grand Lodge; which was adopted.

P. G. C's Rathbone and Barton, and P. C. Carrigan were appointed a committee to have the Grand and Subordinate Lodge installation work printed.

P. C. Kronheimer offered the following resolutions, which were laid over according to rule:

Resolved, That no brother who is not in possession of the quarterly password shall be admitted to a seat, nor gain admittance to a sister Lodge.

Resolved, That hereafter all applicants for membership to the Knights of Pythias shall sign their names to the application, and if they are not competent to do so, they shall not be admitted to fellowship, and those now belonging to the Order who cannot write their names shall be disqualified from ever holding office in the Order.

On motion, and at the request of P. G. C. Rathbone, he was empowered to reorganize Washington Lodge, No. 1, by bringing it back into the Order in a constitutional form.

P. G. C's Rathbone, Barton, and G. C. Dunn were, on motion of P. C. CARRIGAN, appointed a Committee to set to music the Initiatory Anthem.

A communication was read from Franklin Lodge, No. 2, presenting to the Grand Lodge their old Second and Third Degree work. The communication was received, and a vote of thanks tendered that Lodge.

Representative DARNELL offered the following amendment to the Grand Lodge Constitution:

Article 4, Section 1, "That this Grand Lodge hold an annual session on the fourth Tuesday in July."

Representative STROMBERGER moved that the proceedings of the "Old Grand Lodge" be declared null and void, and a committee of three be appointed to procure a new seal.

P. C. D. CARRIGAN moved to lay it on the table, which motion was lost. After debate on the question, P. C. John W. Cross moved to postpone the matter until the second meeting night in August; which was adopted by a vote of fourteen to four.

A debate was here sprung in regard to the expulsion of P. G. C. J. T. K. Plant, and rank of P. G. C. Rathbone.

P. C. WESTWOOD offered the following resolution:

Resolved, That notwithstanding any action to the contrary, V. G. P. J. H. Rathbone is hereby declared to be the senior Past Grand Chancellor of the Order.

The resolution was adopted.

P. C. JOHN H. KING offered the following resolution:

Resolved, That during installation, initiation, and conferring of degrees all other business must be suspended, and no brother will be permitted to enter or retire from the Lodge room.

Also a resolution establishing the mode of balloting. Laid over according to rule. The voting sign of the Order was then established ; and a new form of quarterly reports.

P. G. C. Barton stated that he had been for some time communicating with gentlemen in Philadelphia in relation to establishing the

Order in that city, and was satisfied, from the tenor of their letters, that a Lodge of the Order could be organized there with good material. He asked an appropriation of money to proceed to Philadelphia at once, for the purpose of explaining the principles of the Order to those in that city who were willing to take hold of the matter and to arrange preliminaries previous to their making application for a charter.

On motion the sum of $20 was appropriated from the fund collected by P. C. Hamilton for the payment of P. G. C. Barton's expenses to Philadelphia—and the following Past Chancellors deputized to proceed to Philadelphia in case Brother Barton's efforts were successful: P. G. C. Rathbone, G. C. Edw. Dunn, P. C.'s John W. Cross and Daniel Carrigan.

On motion of P. G. C. RATHBONE, the Subordinate Lodges were requested to turn out in procession, and escort the Grand Officers to the depot on the occasion. The Grand Lodge members were also requested to turn out, and the following committee appointed to procure music: P. G. C. Rathbone and P. C's Childs and King.

P. C. J. W. Cross asked to be excused from serving on the Grievance Committee; which was agreed to.

The following appropriations were made :

Officers' Emblems	$16 00
Deficiency on printed Constitutions	3 00
Blank notices for G. R. S.	4 00
Total	$23 00

Adjourned.

P. G. C. Barton left Washington on the 15th for Philadelphia. On arriving there he proceeded directly to several friends in the northwestern part of that city, and after a consultation upon the subject, they determined to organize a Lodge. A meeting was called at the residence of George Hensler, Esq., corner 15th and Brown Streets, who was chosen its chairman. The objects and principles of the Order were duly explained, and those present subscribed to the application. The name of the Lodge was fixed upon as Excelsior Lodge, No. 1, and the application was forwarded to the Grand Chancellor at Washington.

FEBRUARY 21, 1867.

A special session was held—G. C. Edw. Dunn in the Chair, who stated that he had received a letter from P. G. C. Barton in Philadelphia, informing him of the success he had met with, and also enclosing the following application for a charter; which was read by G. R. S. *pro tempore* D. Carrigan:

PHILADELPHIA, February 19, 1867.

To the G. C. and Members of the Grand Lodge,

Knights of Pythias, D. C.:

The undersigned, residing in the city of Philadelphia, respectfully petition your honorable body to grant them a charter, or dispensation, to establish a Lodge of the Knights of Pythias, to be located in the 15th ward, Philadelphia, said Lodge to be known as Excelsior Lodge, No. 1, Knights of Pythias, and under your jurisdiction.

Charter fee enclosed—$10.

WILBUR H. MYERS............................*Venerable Patriarch,*
FRED. COPPES.....................................*Worthy Chancellor,*
JOHN JAY FISHER.............................*Vice Chancellor,*
WILLIAM A. PORTER..........................*Banker,*
A. J. HUNTZINGER.............................*Financial Scribe,*
G. GRAEF...*Recording "*
J. W. HENCILL..................................*Guide,*
JAMES McDEVITT............................*Inner Steward,*
JAMES HERMANN.............................*Outer "*

George Hensler, Wm. A. McCoy, Wm. R. Buddy, James Culbertson, C. Umstead, Jacob Allen, D. P. Miller, George C. Johnson, C. S. Williams, Robert Jeandelle, Samuel C. Barton, Wm. Allen, Louis Lampter, James Porter, P. Bodamer, P. J. Hallowell, Enoch McCabe, James Dunn, George W. Lauster.

The application was referred to the following committee for examination: P. C's Childs, Smith, and Scott, who reported favorable; when, upon motion, the charter was granted.

On motion it was resolved that the degree work presented to the Grand Lodge by Franklin Lodge, No. 2, be taken to Philadelphia and left in charge of Excelsior Lodge. A committee of one from each Lodge was also appointed to get everything in readiness, and it was resolved that those deputized on the 12th instant to proceed to Philadelphia, leave for that city on the 11:15 train, Saturday, February 23.

Adjourned.

P. G. C. Rathbone, P. C's Carrigan, Cross, Smith, and others were escorted to the depot from Mount Vernon Lodge room, on the morning of the 23d of February, by Heald's Band and the members of the Order in regalia.

On arriving in Philadelphia, they were met by P. G. C. Barton and G. C. Dunn, (who had arrived two days before), and along with their Philadelphia friends proceeded to the Hall of the Mechanic Fire Company, Brown Street, below 15th Street, and there organized Excelsior Lodge, No. 1, and installed their officers on the evening of the 23d of February, 1867.

FEBRUARY 26, 1867.

An adjourned quarterly session was held—P. C. Kronheimer in the chair.

The committee to organize Excelsior Lodge, of Philadelphia, reported the result of their labors, and were discharged from the further consideration of the subject.

The Committee on Music made a partial report, and were granted further time.

On motion of Representative GARRETT, of No. 5, the motion by which the report of the Grievance Committee on the interrogatories of Representative Herrell was laid over until the next session, was reconsidered; and, after debate, the committee's report on the second interrogatory was stricken out, and their report on the first—that no tax could be levied—was adopted as the sense of the Grand Lodge.

The G. R. S. was authorized to forward a communication to No. 5 Lodge, informing them of the illegality of levying the tax of $1 upon their members on the decease of one of their brothers.

A communication was also ordered to be sent to P. C. T. W. Cook, in Philadelphia, requesting him to visit Excelsior Lodge and instruct its members in the work of the Order.

The following resolution, offered by P. G. C. BARTON was adopted :

Resolved, That the Grand Lodge, District of Columbia, shall pay the travelling expenses of one Past Officer of Excelsior Lodge, of Pennsylvania, to attend the Grand Lodge sessions for one year.

P. C. I. L. BLOUT offered a substitute for P. C. King's resolution in regard to the mode of balloting; which was adopted.

An appeal was read from Brothers F. Stromberger and J. T. Roland, of No. 5, protesting against a fine being levied upon them for conversing in the Lodge room during initiation. Referred to the following committee : P. C's Henry, I. L. Blout, and Westwood.

A card of thanks was tendered the members of Excelsior Lodge, Philadelphia, for their kind and generous treatment of the Grand Lodge Delegates while in that city.

Also one to Representative Stromberger for the aid he had given the brethren in preparing the necessary work.

And a card of thanks to the Subordinate Lodges for their turn out on the occasion of escorting the delegates to the depot.

On motion, P. C. John H. King was loaned the emblems of the Grand Lodge, to be used by Franklin Lodge, No. 2, on the occasion of visiting a fair at Odd-Fellows' Hall.

P. G. C. RATHBONE moved that a committee of five be appointed to take into consideration the feasibility of erecting a Hall in the city, to be known as the Hall of the Knights of Pythias; adopted, and the following committee appointed: P. G. C. Rathbone, and P. C's King, Childs, Westwood, and Kronheimer.

The Grand Lodge then adjourned until March 12th.

MARCH 12, 1867.

An adjourned quarterly session was held—G. C. Edward Dunn in the chair.

The credentials of P. C. Wilbur H. Myers, and Reps. Fred. Coppes, Wm. A. Porter. and John W. Hencill, of Excelsior Lodge, Pa., were presented and referred to the Committee on Election and Returns; which reported favorable.

Reps. Coppes and Porter were then introduced and instructed.

The Committee on Music made a report, and requested an appropriation of $5 to supply deficiency.

On motion of P. C. J. S. Martin, the report was received, and the request granted; the Committee was then discharged.

An application for a card was read from J. N. Turpin, a former member of Washington Lodge, No. 1, and referred to P. C's Johnson, Kronheimer, and Carrigan.

The By-Laws of Excelsior Lodge, of Pennsylvania, were presented, read, and approved, and that Lodge empowered to keep open its charter books until the first meeting in July.

The Committee on Printing Installation Work of Grand and Subordinate Lodges was empowered to have 100 copies printed.

The Committee on Supervision were, on motion of P. C. KING, ordered to report at the next session all conflictions between the Ritual and Constitution.

APPROPRIATION.—$5.00 to Committee on Music.

Adjourned.

REGULAR QUARTERLY SESSION.

APRIL 9, 1867.

The Grand Lodge assembled in quarterly session, and was opened in due form—G. C. Edward Dunn in the chair. Prayer by V. G. P. pro tem. Carrigan.

The proceedings of the adjourned and special sessions were read and approved.

The Committee on Election and Returns reported favorably on the returns of Nos. 2, 5 and 6, of D. C., and No. 1, of Philadelphia. The returns of No. 7, of D. C., were not presented.

The credentials of the following Brothers were found correct, and so reported by the Committee; P. C's W. H. Myers, of Pa.; C. Hutzler, of No. 2; B. Daughton, of No. 5; James Matthieson, No. 6; Jacob Peyser, No. 7, and Reps. Allen, McInturff, and Gordon, of No. 6, and Okey, Cole, and Nattans, of No. 7.

The following, being present, were admitted and instructed: P. C's Myers, Hutzler, Matthieson, and Daughton, and Reps. Allen, McInturff, and Cole.

. The Committee to whom was referred the application of J. N. Turpin for a card, made an unfavorable report, finding that at the time of the decease of Washington Lodge the Brother was not in good standing. The report was received and the Committee discharged.

The Committee on Grievance, to whom was referred the appeal of Bros. Stromberger and Roland, of No. 5, reported that the cause of the Brothers being fined was of such a nature that it would not justify a fine, and that the Brothers were fined contrary to custom and law, there being no legal charges brought against them for the offence at the time. The report was received and adopted, and the committee discharged.

Applications for cards from T. Harry Donahue, of late Washington Lodge, and John P. Lucas, of late Potomac Lodge, were read and referred to the following committee: P. C's Fox, Matthieson, and Daughton.

An application for card was also received from Isaac N. Bowen, a Past Chancellor of late Alexandria Lodge; which, on the recommendation of P. C. Jno. H. King, was granted.

A communication was read from Excelsior Lodge, of Philadelphia, informing the Grand Lodge of the election of their officers for the ensuing quarter. Also, one tendering the thanks of their Lodge to the Grand Lodge for the generous treatment of their Representatives at the last Grand Lodge session.

And one from Franklin Lodge, No. 2, notifying the Grand Lodge that fifty additional members had been secured by that Lodge, according to the rules prescribed by the Grand Lodge. Also, one from same Lodge, notifying the Grand Lodge of P. C's who were in arrears.

The communications were received and noted.

On motion, the action of Excelsior Lodge, in re-electing the same officers for the ensuing quarter, was sustained.

An appeal was read from A. F. Altemus, of No. 7 Lodge, claiming that H. V. Cole had been unconstitutionally elected Financial Scribe of that Lodge, and that he (Altemus) was entitled to the office; referred to the Grievance Committee.

The amendments to the Grand Lodge Constitution—offered by P. G. C. C. M. Barton, and Rep. Darnell, on the 29th January—were then taken up and adopted—making the time for holding the quarterly session on the 2d Tuesday of each quarter, and the annual session on the 4th Tuesday in July.

The resolutions of P. C. H. KRONHEIMER, proposing an amendment to the Grand Lodge constitution, which were presented on 12th February, were taken up and, after discussion, were rejected.

The amendment offered by Rep. Stromberger, that "No Brother shall be eligible to the office of W. C. until he has served one term in each subordinate office, commencing with the office of Financial Scribe, and progressing upward," was taken up and, after lengthy debate, adopted. A vote by lodges being called, resulted as follows: Affirmative—Mount Vernon, Webster, Excelsior; Negative—Franklin and Liberty.

The following committee was appointed to devise a P. C's and Rep's Degree for the Grand Lodge: G. C. Edward Dunn, P. G. C. C. M. Barton, and P. C's Myers, Childs, Westwood, and Kronheimer.

The following committee was appointed to inquire into the expediency of giving an excursion for the benefit of the Grand Lodge: P. G. C. Barton, and P. C's Childs and Kronheimer.

The following appropriations were made:

Installation Work (printing)	$26 00
Hall Rent	4 89
C. M. Barton, travelling expenses	10 00
W. H. Myers, " "	10 00
Total	50 89

RECEIPTS.

Per centage from Subordinate Lodges	$99 70
Cards	4 50
Total	$104 20

The Grand Lodge then adjourned.

Table showing the condition of the Lodges at the close of the first quarter ending March 31, 1867.

Names.	Membership.							Received during quarter.				Expended during quarter.				On hand.				Per Centage to Grand Lodge.
	Increase.	Decrease.	Pages.	Esquires.	Knights.	P. C.'s.	P.G. C.'s.	General fund.	School or Widow and Orphan Fund.	Special tax.	Total.	Relief of sick.	Funerals.	Relief of distress.	Total expended.	General fund.	Widow and orphan or school fund.	Special tax.	Total on hand.	
No. 2, Franklin	19	1			78	13	2	$193 29	$21 81	$48 53	$363 60	$24 70		$10 00	$189 00	$225 41	$52 09	$48 50	$276 60	$19 02
No. 5, Mount Vernon	10	6	5	3	91	5		237 29	26 38	92 25	355 90				248 22	247 54	65 14		347 68	23 7?
No. , Liberty	17		7	7	102	5		334 16	38 57	156 93	529 68				331 46	400 59	230 21		660 80	23 41
No. 7. Webster	7		1	1	34	4		64 73	7 19		71 92				79 25	28 38	25 00		61 38	6 4?
No. 1, (Pa.), Excelsior			1	1	51	1		164 75	18 30		183 05				45 66	100 79	18 70		119 09	16 47
	53 7		13	11	416	28	2	$997 22	$112 23	$297 70	$1407 15	$24 70		$10 00	$853 60	$1002 71	$461 34	$43 50	$1512 55	65 70

Total Membership 470.

MAY 14, 1867.

A special session was held—Grand Banker Jno. H. King in the chair.

On motion, the vote by which the amendment of Rep. Stromberger to the Constitution was effected at the last session, was declared null and void, the vote on the amendment having been taken by Lodges, when Article XVIII of the Grand Lodge Constitution required all amendments to be approved by a vote of two-thirds of the members present entitled to vote, before they became a part of the Constitution.

The committee on the application of John P. Lucas for card, made a favorable report, and a card was granted.

The Committee on Supervision reported conflictions between the Ritual and Constitution.

The Committee on Grievances reported upon the appeal of A. F. Altemus, that he was entitled to the office of Financial Scribe, and that Brother Cole* was not.

The reports were received and adopted.

Bro. John Meyer, formerly a member of the late Potomac Lodge, applied for a card, and P. C's Westwood, Johnson, and Childs were appointed a committee upon it.

Receipts.—Card of John Meyer, $1.50.

The Grand Lodge then adjourned.

JUNE 17, 1867.

A special session was held—G. C. Edward Dunn in the chair.

An application for a charter to organize Columbia Lodge, No. 8, was presented, accompanied with the charter fee and requisite number of signers—the Lodge to be located in the southwestern part of the city of Washington, D. C. The application was dated May 10, 1867, and signed as follows: Wm. H. Signor, Geo. H. Kepplar, James T. Davis, Wm. T. Hall, Geo. W. Sewell, James B. Shearer, G. W. Barkman, J. H. Truett, and J. R. N. Curtin. The application was received, referred to the appropriate committee, which reported favorably, and the charter granted; previous to which the name of Columbia was stricken out, and the applicants ordered to be informed that the name of Washington or Columbia could not be used by a new Lodge, there being two defunct Lodges bearing those names.

Receipts.—Charter fee, $10.00

The Grand Lodge then adjourned.

---

*At the beginning of the quarter, Brother H. V. Cole was installed into office by the Grand Chancellor, the objections to the contrary notwithstanding.

JUNE 25, 1867.

A special session was held for the purpose of organizing Friendship Lodge, No. 8—G. C. Edward Dunn in the chair. A committee was appointed to wait on the applicants and procure a list of their officers. The committee reported the following: V. G. P. (past officer) J. R. N. Curtin ; Worthy Chancellor John H. Kepplar ; V. C. Geo. W. Sewell ; Banker, James Shearer ; R. S. W. T. Hall ; F. S. W. H. Signor ; Guide, L. B. Grimes ; I. S. Jas. L. Davis ; O. S. Geo. W. Barkman. The above officers and several members were then introduced and instructed in the mysteries of the several degrees.
Adjourned.

REGULAR QUARTERLY SESSION.

JULY 9, 1867.

The Grand Lodge assembled in due form—G. C. Dunn in the chair. Prayer by V. G. P. *pro tem.* Edward Fox.

The minutes of the last quarterly and special sessions were read and approved.

The Committee on Election and Returns reported the returns of Nos. 2 and 6 correct, and those of No. 1, of Pa., and Nos. 5 and 7, of D.C., incorrect—the former not having the W. C's signature attached, and the two latter having no seals affixed. The report was received and adopted by vote of 18 to 3.

The credentials of the Past Chancellors and Representatives were then examined by the committee, and the following were admitted and instructed. P. C's John Schultz, No. 2 ; J. R. N. Curtin, No. 8 ; F. Wood, No. 5 ; A. Shaw, No. 6 : C. W. Okey, No. 7 ; Reps. Allen, McInturff, and Garrett, No. 6 ; Wilbourne, Dykes, and Kepplar, No. 8 ; and Cole, Clark, and Altemus, of No. 7.

The following committees, being unable to report, were discharged : On Regalia, Excursion, and Degree Work.

A communication was read from Excelsior Lodge, of Pennsylvania, asking the Grand Lodge to confer the Past Chancellor's Degree upon all of their first installed officers, in order to advance the work in Philadelphia ; that they be empowered to make their R. S., B., and O. S. yearly officers, and that they be empowered to hold a new election for officers to serve the balance of the quarter. Ordered to be recorded.

P. G. C. BARTON offered the following :

Whereas Excelsior Lodge, No. 1, of Philadelphia, organized but little more than four months since, and now numbering 300 members, in order to more fully carry on the work begun in Philadelphia, have respectfully made application to this Grand Lodge for a dispensation to make their first officers Past Officers ; and whereas the Grand Lodge of D. C., fully recognizing the great interest Excelsior Lodge has taken in endeavoring to spread the Order, and desiring to extend to them all the facilities in our power for so doing : Therefore be it

Resolved, That John Jay Fisher, Wm. H. Wartman, Geo. W. Pugh, Wm. A. Porter, John W. Hencill, James McDevitt, Jos. Hermann, and John Brown, M. D., be, and they are hereby, declared to be Past Chancellors of the Knights of Pythias, of the State of Pennsylvania, entitled to all the amenities and privileges of Past Chancellors of the Order.

On motion, the rules were suspended to take up the resolution. An amendment was offered to insert after the names, the names of the Recording Scribes and Bankers of Nos. 5, 6, 7, and 8 Lodges, which was laid on the table. The resolution then passed, after debate, by a vote of 17 to 7.

On motion, Friendship Lodge, No. 8, was allowed to keep open their charter six months from its date.

A communication was read from Union Lodge, No. 11, I. O. O. F., instructing the Grand Lodge to turn over all money for hall rent to Parker Hall Sweet, Secretary of the Grand Lodge of Odd-Fellows, until further orders.

Communications were read from Mount Vernon Lodge—one requesting a new First Degree Work, in lieu of the one taken by the Grand Officers to Philadelphia, and one requesting a charter from the Grand Lodge, in lieu of the one granted by the Past Chancellors of Franklin Lodge. The requests contained in the communications were granted.

Representative GARRETT offered the following:

Resolved. That Article 6, Section 9, requiring elective officers of Subordinate Lodges to serve in the capacity of O. S., and progress upward to the Chair of W. C., be annulled, and insert "from Financial Scribe."

A motion was made to suspend the rules, to take up the resolution; which was laid on the table. The resolution was laid over.

Rep. ALLEN offered the following:

Resolved, That Recording Scribe, Theodore Sniffin, of Liberty Lodge, No. 6, Knights of Pythias, be, and is hereby entitled to receive the Grand Lodge Degree.

The resolution was taken up, discussed, and then laid upon the table.

Several amendments to the Grand Lodge Constitution were then offered by P. G. C. BARTON, and laid over.

The Grand Lodge then went into nominations for Grand Officers with the following result:

For Grand Chancellor: P. C's Westwood, Carrigan, Childs, King, and P. G. C. Barton; for Vice Grand Chancellor: P. C's Carrigan, Kronheimer, Smith, Johnson, Sears, and King; for Grand Recording Scribe: P. C's Westwood and Okey, and P. G. C. Barton; for Grand Financial Scribe: P. C's Cross, Okey, Curtin, Wood, and Johnson; for Grand Banker: P. C's Martin, Westwood, and G. C. Dunn; for Grand Guide: Cross, Wood, Sears, Johnson, Okey, Kronheimer, and Curtin; for Grand Inner Steward: P. C's Westwood, Wood, Childs, Sears, and P. G. C. Barton; for Grand Outer Steward: P. C. Martin and P. G. C. Barton.

On motion of P. G. C. BARTON, a committee on printing was appointed with full power to have all necessary printing done for the Order. P. G. C. Barton, P. C. Carrigan, and P. C. Okey, Committee.

RECEIPTS................ $65 21   EXPENDITURES—for hall rent, $9 37.

The Grand Lodge then adjourned.

Report showing the condition of the Lodges at the end of the Quarter and Year, June 30, 1867.

Names	Membership							Received during quarter.				Expended during quarter.				On hand.				Per Centage to Grand Lodge.
	Increase.	Decrease.	Pages.	Esquires.	Knights.	P. C's.	P. G. C's.	General Fund.	School or Widow and Orphan Fund.	Special Tax.	Total.	Relief of Sick.	Funerals.	Relief of Distress.	Total Expended.	General Fund.	Widow and Orphan, or School Fund.	Special Tax.	Total on hand.	
No. 2, Franklin	10	1	10	1	81	14	1	$151.73	$16.85	$49.75	$218.33	$16.00			$90.37	$385.26	$79.54	$40.75	$494.55	$15.17
No. 5, Mount Vernon	7	2	5	4	94	6		155.21	17.24	81.16	253.61	36.00			104.93	378.98	82.39		461.33	15.52
No. 6, Liberty	11	4	6	7	171	5		283.62	31.51	140.75	455.88	52.00			345.76	479.70	324.72		804.42	28.38
No. 7, Webster	8	2			40	1		67.78	6.77		74.55								70.12	0.16
No. 8, Friendship					16	2											87.49		28.06	
No. 1 (Pa.), Excelsior	109	9	9	22	100	2		622.76	69.19		691.95				283.28	412.77			500.25	62.27
	235	9	30	32	598	33	1	$1281.10	$141.56	$271.66	$1694.32	104.00			$794.34	$1636.71	$574.13	$49.75	$2358.71	$127.48

Total Membership 694.

JULY 15, 1867.

A special session was held—G. C. Edw. Dunn in the chair.

An application for a charter for Keystone Lodge, No. 2, of Philadelphia was received, dated June 29, 1867—charter fee enclosed, and twenty-six signatures attached.

On motion of P. C. D. CARRIGAN the charter was granted, and P. C. Harry Kronheimer deputized to proceed to Philadelphia on the following Thursday and install the officers and initiate the members of the new Lodge.

RECEIPTS—Charter fee.. $10 00
EXPENDITURES—Travelling expenses to H. Kronheimer................ 10 00

Adjourned.

ANNUAL SESSION.

JULY 23, 1867.

The Grand Lodge assembled and was opened in due form.

PRESENT: J. H. RATHBONE.................... *Venerable Grand Patriarch,*
　　　　　EDW. DUNN......................... *Grand Chancellor,*
　　　　　C. M. BARTON...................... *Grand Recording Scribe,*
　　　　　WM. L. CHILDS..................... *Grand Financial Scribe,*
　　　　　JOHN H. KING...................... *Grand Banker,*
　　　　　WM. P. WESTWOOD.................. *Grand Guide,*
　　　　　R. T. JOHNSON..................... *Grand Inner Steward.*

Prayer by V. G. P. J. H. Rathbone.

The proceedings of the regular quarterly and special sessions were read and approved.

The credentials of P. C's Coppes, Wm. A. Porter, and Reps. Wallace, Curry, and Ashe, of Excelsior Lodge, No. 1, of Philadelphia, were found correct, and the Brothers admitted and instructed.

The Committee on Printing reported having procured 200 copies blank Quarterly Reports, 200 odes, and 100 withdrawal cards. The report was received.

The report of the Finance Committee was, upon motion of P. C. R. T. JOHNSON, laid over until the adjourned session, and Rep. Allen, of No. 6, appointed to serve upon the committee, in place of P. C. Childs, who declined—the committee now standing as follows: P. G. C. Rathbone and P. C. Scott and Rep. Allen.

An application for a charter for Chosen Friends Lodge, No. 3, of Philadelphia, dated July 20, 1867, was then read—charter fee enclosed, and signed by the requisite number.

The charter was unanimously granted, and the G. C. appointed D.

G. C. W. H. Myers, P. C's Coppes, Porter, and Hencill, of Pennsylvania, and G. G. Kronheimer, of D. C., to initiate and install the new Lodge.

On motion of P. C. COPPES, Keystone Lodge, No. 2, was empowered to keep open their charter until October 26, 1867.

P. C. R. T. JOHNSON moved that the action of the Grand Lodge in February last, (26th,) declaring illegal the action of Mount Vernon Lodge, in levying the $1 tax upon its members, in the case of the death of a Brother, be repealed. After considerable debate upon the subject, the motion was adopted.

P. C. C. W. OKEY moved the nomination of officers be re-opened: lost.

On motion of P. C. J. S. MARTIN the Grand Lodge went into an election for officers for the ensuing year. P. C's Porter and Coppes, of No. 1, Pa., were appointed tellers.

P. G. C. Barton withdrew his name for the office of Grand Chancellor, and the first ballot resulted as follows, viz: Carrigan, 14; Westwood, 14; Childs, 7; King, 3—no choice. P. C's Childs and King withdrew their names. Second ballot: Westwood, 22; Carrigan, 16; necessary to a choice, 20. P. C. Westwood was therefore declared elected Grand Chancellor.

For Vice Grand Chancellor, P. C's Smith and King withdrew their names, and the ballot resulted as follows: Carrigan, 19; Kronheimer, 10; Johnson, 7. P. C. Carrigan was declared elected Vice Grand Chancellor.

For Grand Recording Scribe, P. G. C. C. M. Barton was unanimously elected. There being no opposition candidate, P. G. C. Rathbone cast the vote of the Lodge.

Grand Financial Scribe—First ballot: Cross, 8; Okey, 13; Wood, 9—no choice. Second ballot: Cross, 10; Okey, 13; Wood, 8—no choice. P. C. Wood withdrew his name. Third ballot: Okey, 19; Cross, 12. P. C. Okey was declared elected Grand Financial Scribe.

For Grand Banker, P. G. C. Dunn withdrew his name, and there being but one nominee—P. C. J. S. Martin—he was declared unanimously elected. There being no opposing candidate, P. G. C. Rathbone cast the vote for the Grand Lodge.

Grand Guide, P. C. Sears, withdrew his name. First ballot: Cross, 4; Wood, 6; Kronheimer, 12; Curtin, 5—no choice. Second ballot—P. C. Curtin withdrew—Cross, 4; Wood, 8; Kronheimer, 14. P. C. Kronheimer was declared elected Grand Guide.

For Grand Inner Steward—Wood, 17; Childs, 1. P. C. Wood was declared elected.

For Grand Outer Steward, the following nominations were made : P. G. C. Rathbone and P. C. Lawson. The vote stood as follows : P. G. C. Rathbone, 11 ; P. C. Lawson, 13. The latter was declared duly elected.

G. C. Dunn then installed his successor, who, in turn, installed the remaining newly-elected officers.

On motion of P. G. C. RATHBONE the thanks of the Grand Lodge were tendered to the late Grand Chancellor, for his efficiency during the past year. •

Several amendments to the Ritual were then offered by P. G. C. Barton, and laid over according to rule.

The case of Croton Fletcher was also disposed of, by empowering any Lodge in the District to initiate and confer the three Degrees upon him for five dollars.

The following rates of tariff, for Grand Lodge Revenue, were determined upon :

Withdrawal cards, each...	25
Odes, each..	5
Ritual—1st set..	$20 00
" 2d set...	10 00
Installation Work, per set...	1 50

The following resolution was offered and adopted :

Resolved, That members of defunct Lodges who were not in good standing at the time of the decease of their Lodge, and who apply for admission into the Order, can receive a card from this Grand Lodge by paying the amount standing against them upon the books of their respective Lodges.

The Grand Lodge adjourned until August 15.

RECEIPTS.

Chosen Friends Lodge, No. 3, Pa., charter fee.........................	$10 00
Excelsior Lodge, No. 1, Pa., percentage...............................	62 27
" " " Rituals..	20 00
Total..	92 27

APPROPRIATIONS.

To Printing Committee...	$30 00
C. M. Barton, services..	25 00
P. C. F. Coppes, of Pa., travelling expenses.........................	10 00
Total..	65 00

During the year the Lodges had paid to the Grand Lodge as per centage......	$389 77
The total receipts for the year were................................	576 79
Total expended..	347 01

Leaving a balance in hands of newly elected Banker of...$229 78

The Order now numbered eight Lodges, namely, Franklin, No. 2; Mount Vernon, No. 5; Liberty, No. 6; Webster, No. 7, and Friendship, No. 8, of the District of Columbia, and Excelsior, Keystone, and Chosen Friends, of Philadelphia.

The quarterly report of No. 1 Lodge, of Philadelphia, showed that the experiment of planting the Order outside of the District had by no means been a failure; but, on the contrary, its principles seemed to be disseminated as if by magic, and those who embraced them, saw, by the very simplicity of the work, and the practical lessons taught by the Ritual, a glorious future for the Order in the State of Pennsylvania and elsewhere.

CLARENCE M. BARTON, P. G. C.,
Grand Recording Scribe.

SUSPENSIONS.

Upon the 1st day of July, 1867, the following members stood sus·pended: Franklin Lodge, No. 2—J. T. K. Plant, J. V. Wannell, F. C. Dell, for non-payment of dues, and George M. Norton and James E. Gill for contempt to the Lodge.

Mount Vernon Lodge, No. 5—G. W. Crutchley, Edw. Godfrey, Samuel Hays, James Lomax, John Simms, Samuel C. Hunt, Richard Dawes, M D., for non-payment of dues, and John W. Meed for drunkenness.

Webster Lodge, No. 7—L. Gassenheimer and Joseph Gatto for non·payment of dues.

OFFICERS.

Term Expiring July, 1868.

EDW. DUNN.............................. *Venerable Grand Patriarch,*
WM. P. WESTWOOD.................... *Grand Chancellor,*
DANIEL CARRIGAN.................. *Vice Grand Chancellor,*
CLARENCE M. BARTON................ *Grand Recording Scribe,*
C. W. OKEY............................. " *Financial Scribe,*
JOSEPH S. MARTIN.................... " *Banker,*
HARRY KRONHEIMER.................. " *Guide,*
FRANCIS WOOD....................... " *Inner Steward,*
RICHARD LAWSON..................... " *Outer Steward.*

Residence of Grand Chancellor—Georgia Avenue, bet. 3d and 4th Streets, East.

Residence of Grand Recording Scribe—9th Street East, one door below E Street South, Washington, D. C.

ADDENDA.

The original meeting, when the work of the Order of the Knights of Pythias was first read, took place at the house No. 369 F Street, between 8th and 9th Streets; the following gentlemen being present, (as the members of a musical association known as the " Arion Glee Club:") Messrs. R. A. Champion, E. S. Kimball, D. L. Burnett, W. H. Burnett, Roberts, and Driver. Each of these gentlemen were then and there duly obligated by Mr. Rathbone, and afterwards re-solved themselves into individual committees to obtain the names of proper persons to form the first Lodge. This meeting took place Monday Evening, February 15, 1864, and on the following Wednes·day morning Mr. Rathbone informed Mr. J. T. K. Plant of the object of the meeting, and solicited him to join the Order. Mr. Rathbone had, however, read the Ritual to Mr. R. A. Champion, privately, at his own room, a few evenings previous to the above meeting.

The Ritual was written by Mr. J. H. Rathbone, originally, in the town of Eagle Harbor, Houghton (now Keewenaw) County, Lake Superior, Michigan, in the winter of 1860 and 1861.